Jon Blake

illustrated by
David Roberts

*Hodder
Children's
Books*

A division of Hodder Headline Limited

Before We Begin

First let me introduce myself. I am Blue Soup. I tell stories. I also light up cities, provide hot dinners, and make that little thing in the top of the toilet go FZZZZZZZ. In fact, I make everything work, so no one has to waste their time being a cleaner, or an estate agent, or an MP.

What am I, you ask? Well, I'm not a person, that's obvious. Or a team of people. Or a computer virus. But please don't waste your time trying to imagine me, because you can't, just like you can't imagine the end of time, or what's beyond the very last star. If you do try to imagine me, first you will get a headache, then your head will explode.

As you've probably guessed, I come from Outer Space. Beyond the very last star, in fact. I was brought here by what you call aliens, except to them, you are aliens, and pretty weird ones at that.

Anyway, enough of me. This is the second story of Stinky Finger, who I first described in Stinky Finger's House of Fun. He definitely isn't an alien. He talks like a human, walks like a human, and smells like a dead fish.

Chapter One

Stinky Finger and Icky Bats were reliving their greatest memories of life in the House of Fun.

"Remember when the house was under siege from the army of pigs?" asked Stinky.

"Yeah," said Icky, "and we went back into the past, and brought back a dinosaur egg, and it hatched into a dinosaur, and we rode it at the pigs, and they ran away, all except General Pig, who ran into the house and turned into a potato."

"Yes," said Stinky. "But you shouldn't use too many 'and's when telling a story. Bryan said."

A bother-frown appeared on Icky's face. "Whatever happened to Bryan?" he asked.

"That's a point," replied Stinky. "We haven't seen him in ages."

Icky and Stinky tried to remember where they'd last seen Bryan, the brainy know-it-all accident-prone bighead who also lived in the House of Fun.

"The last time *I* remember seeing him," said Stinky, "we were playing Sardines, and he'd gone off to hide."

"Ah yes," said Icky. "Then something came through the door, and we went off to see what it was."

"How could anything come through the door?" asked Stinky. "The mailbox is at the gate."

"Don't you remember?" said Icky. "I made a letterbox, because the mailbox was full of your Uncle Nero's head."

"Ah yes," said Stinky.

The two great mates fell into a long silent ponder.

"Did we ever find out what came through the door?" asked Stinky.

"No," said Icky. "One of Dronezone had rolled into the hall, so we went to put him back on the sofa. Then they got excited and started singing, so we listened to them for a few hours, by which time it was tea-time."

Dronezone, of course, were the top-ten boy band who had turned into potatoes after watching TV in the Living Living Room, one of the many weird rooms in the House of Fun. They didn't often sing these days, which was why Icky and Stinky had bothered to listen to them.

"I wonder what it *was* that came through the door," mused Stinky.

"Let's find out now!" cried Icky, leaping up. Icky was like that. He had lots of sudden ideas and was forever leaping up, down and generally all over the place. Stinky, on the other hand, never leapt anywhere, mainly because his mouldy trousers stuck to whatever he was sitting on.

As usual, Icky helped Stinky to his feet, because Icky was a very good friend to Stinky. They set off for the front door, hoping nothing would distract them. That was the problem with the House of Fun. There was always *something* to divert you, unless you were very careful, which Icky and Stinky weren't.

"I shall be interested to see the front door," said Stinky. "How many days is it since we went outside?"

Icky counted on his fingers. "Three ... five ... seven ... eight ... nine," he muttered. "That's it. Nine months."

"I wonder if anything has changed," said Stinky.

"Remember when we first came here," said Icky, "and there was snow all over the city, and we saw the house on its own little hill, and found your uncle—"

"Icky," interrupted Stinky.

"What?" said Icky.

"You're saying too many 'and's again," said Stinky.

"I *like* saying 'and'," said Icky, then stopped. "Bryan!" he said. "We were going to look for Bryan!"

"Oh yeah," said Stinky. "Where shall we start?"

"He could be in tenth century China, for all we know," said Icky.

"Didn't we ban the Time Travel Garage?" asked Stinky.

"Ah yes," said Icky. "At least that narrows it down to our own time zone."

Icky and Stinky visited the Kitchen of Magical Invention, the Uninvited Guest Bedroom, the Cheesy Dreams Bedroom, the Undersea World of Uncle Nero Bathroom and the Random Madness Gym. They even took a short peek in the Attic of Horrors, not that Bryan was likely to be there, after his experience with the giant spider.

"He's nowhere," said Stinky.

"He's got to be *somewhere*," said Icky.

"He wouldn't be in ... you know ..." muttered Stinky.

"**Satan's Crypt**?" said Icky.

"Don't say it!" cried Stinky. Stinky preferred not even to think of that dark, doomy place deep beneath the house, the one place the housemates had never dared venture.

"If he's in **Satan's Crypt**," said Icky, "he's staying there."

"There's so many rooms in this house," said Stinky. "Maybe there's one we've forgotten."

"Of course!" cried Icky. "The dressing-up closet! He's *bound* to be in there!"

Bryan had also had a bad experience of the dressing-up closet, but it *was* a very good place to hide. There were rows and rows of costumes on hangers, cupboards crammed with hats and shoes, corners full of tailors' dummies, and even a few props from old stage shows.

Icky's eye fell on one of these. It was the Ancient Egyptian Mummy Casket, which stood at the far end of the room. The first time they'd seen this monstrous object, Icky and Stinky had immediately decided it was cursed. Since then they'd avoided it like the plague.

"Surely Bryan wouldn't have been *that* stupid ..." said Icky.

"You'd have to be a complete *idiot* to get in there," said Stinky.

16

"No, he *couldn't* have been that stupid," said Icky.

"It would have been the *dumbest* thing anyone had ever done in the whole history of the world," said Stinky.

Icky and Stinky nervously approached the casket. With teeth gritted and hearts fluttering, they took hold of the great heavy door. First it wouldn't move at all. Then it gave a little creak. Slowly, agonisingly, it crept open.

There inside, large as life and twice as ugly, was nobody.

"Knew he couldn't have been that stupid," said Icky.

Suddenly there was a loud cry. "For pity's sake!" it went. "Get a move on!"

Icky sprang round, eyes darting all over the place. "That sounded like Bryan!" he cried.

"Of course it's flaming Bryan!" yelled the voice.

Icky and Stinky moved in the direction of the voice, but there was nothing but rails full of costumes. Icky ducked down and checked along the floor, but there was no sign of Bryan's sensible shoes.

"The dog!" cried the voice. "The spotty dog!"

17

Icky and Stinky homed in closer to the voice, thwacking the costumes this way and that, until they finally thwacked something suspiciously heavy which went *Ow*. There indeed was a spotty dog, hanging limply from the clothes rail, with Bryan's eyes peering out of the face.

"Bryan!" said Stinky. "What are you doing there?"

"Hiding from you, stupid!" barked Bryan.

"You're the one that's stupid," snapped Icky, "staying there for three days."

"But it was such a *frabjous* place to hide!" said Bryan. "I wanted you to find me and say, 'What a frabjous place to hide, Bryan!'"

"Frabjous place to hide, Bryan," said Stinky.

"Thank you," said Bryan. "Can you get me down now?"

Icky and Stinky eased the spotty dog off of the rail, and all three collapsed in a heap.

"That's the last time I play Sardines with you two," said Bryan, struggling out of the costume.

"Fine," said Icky. "But in case you forgot, we're your only friends."

A sheepish look came over Bryan, who'd only just got over looking doggish.

"Tell you what," said Stinky. "You can come with us on our exposition to the front door."

"Expedition," corrected Bryan.

The three mates stood at the front door. There on the mat lay a single white card. Icky picked it up and Bryan read it out.

PLEASE GIVE BRAINS

The Brain Donor Van will be in your area on Weds 12 December.

Please be a brain donor.

Giving brains is completely painless and will only take twenty minutes.

Only a small portion of your brain will be taken and this will not noticeably affect your intelligence or normal functions such as the ability to spel.

All brain donors receive a badge saying I'm a Brain Donor – R U?

Your friends,

The Blue Soup Supply Unit (Brains Division)

Icky looked most disappointed. "Is that all?" he said. "I thought it might be something new, exciting and different."

Note from Blue Soup:

After the Spoonheads arrived and sucked all the grown-ups into a space zoo, I (Blue Soup) took over all the boring jobs, as I have already mentioned. If you imagine me as a car, which I'm nothing like, then sunlight is my petrol and dust is my oil. Fortunately there is a fair amount of sunlight and absolutely tons of dust on Earth. However, just as a car also needs that squishy stuff that squirts over the windscreen, I also need human brains. I will still work without them, but I can't see where I'm going, so there is the danger of a major crash.

"Suppose we better do our duty," said Stinky.

"Maybe the van's already been, and we've missed it," said Icky, hopefully.

Bryan checked his state-of-the-art multifunction wrist bangle. "Tuesday December 11th," he confirmed.

"Just our luck," said Stinky. Then he noticed Icky's face, which had suddenly been struck by a mixture of shock and wonderment. "What is it, Icky?" he asked.

"It's ..." stammered Icky.

"Yes?" prompted Stinky.

"It's ..." repeated Icky.

"Yes?" repeated Stinky.

"*Nearly Christmas!*" blurted Icky.

Icky was absolutely right. Christmas was just two weeks away, and the three mates hadn't even realised.

"I love Christmas!" said Bryan. "Mum and Dad always get a *huge* tree, and—"

Bryan stopped, as he remembered that his mum and dad, like all adults, were now somewhere in the Upper Plexian Galaxy. They were most unlikely to get a tree this year, or a cake, or presents for that matter.

"What will we do without grown-ups?" moaned Bryan, who for the first time had realised grown-ups had a use.

"We'll make our own Christmas!" said Icky.

"What, just the three of us?" said Stinky.

It did seem a dismal prospect.

"I know!" said Icky, "we'll turn the House of Fun into a fantastic Christmas grotto, and invite every one of our friends, and have the greatest feast the world has ever seen!"

As usual, Icky's ideas made one part of Stinky very excited, and another part hugely worried. "What if it turns out horribly, horribly wrong?" he asked.

"Nothing can *possibly* go wrong!" said Icky. He seemed the most confident and certain person in the world, which strangely made Stinky twice as worried as before.

Chapter Two

With a sigh of relief, Stinky finished the last of his invitations. Stinky wrote very slowly, partly because he was a slow writer, and partly because he had to keep wiping off the insects and bits of debris which fell out of his hair as he wrote. Icky had finished his own invitations in about two minutes, so now they put the two piles together and counted them. This made a running total of a hundred and thirty-seven guests, which they added to Bryan's invites to make a grand total of ... a hundred and thirty-seven guests.

"Haven't you even got a sister?" asked Icky.

"If I have, I've never noticed her," replied Bryan.

That was just about possible, thought Icky.

Still, even allowing for the fact that Bryan had no friends, relations or close pets, they would have a pretty full house if everyone turned up.

"I'm still not sure about these invitations," said Stinky.

"What's wrong with them?" asked Bryan.

"You don't think they sound a bit ... bigheaded?" asked Stinky.

Bryan re-read the invitations, which (needless to say) he had written himself:

You are cordially invited to
THE BEST CHRISTMAS PARTY EVER
❄ at the BEST HOUSE IN THE UNIVERSE (No. 1, Spatula Drive)
❄ hosted by THE MOST FANTASTIC HOSTS IN HISTORY (Bryan Brain, Icky Bats and Stinky Finger)
❄ on 25th DECEMBER (Christmas)
YOU WILL TALK ABOUT THIS FEAST FOR EVER!
BE THERE OR BE SQUARE!

"Sounds fine to me," said Bryan.

"Unless anything goes wrong, and we end up looking the most biggest idiots in history," said Stinky.

"Just 'biggest' will do," corrected Bryan. "The 'most' is superfluous."

"Eh?" said Stinky.

"Let's just post 'em!" said Icky.

Note from Blue Soup:

You may wonder why the three mates were sending their invitations by post, rather than e-mail, text message, or zip magnet (something invented shortly before the Spoonheads first arrived). The answer is simple. The Spoonheads tended to get stuck in the World Wide Web rather as moths get stuck in spiders' webs. That was why they dissolved it, together with most other forms of electronic communication. They did intend to replace these with safer and more advanced forms, but (as mentioned in my previous volume) were called away unexpectedly. The post was therefore all that survived, although this was now completely operated by postbots controlled by me (Blue Soup).

The three mates set off for the post-hole, which was halfway up the long road which led to the House of Fun. It was a dim drizzly day, where the world was dank and dreary and everything began with D. Just the kind of day for staying indoors, thought Stinky – rather like the past nine months, in fact.

It was lucky the post-hole was not far away. At the end of the street were a gang of dogs, just hanging around looking for trouble. Since the Spoonheads had taught animals to speak, a few had got quite nasty, as Icky and Stinky had already discovered.

"Got a light?" one of the dogs barked.

"We don't smoke," Bryan called back. "It's filthy and unhealthy."

"Bryan!" hissed Stinky. "Shut up!"

But the damage was already done. The dogs were advancing with menace. "What d'you say, mate?" rasped a mean-eyed lurcher.

"Run!" said Icky, and the three mates went full-pelt for the House of Fun, scrabbling up the steps and slamming the door behind them.

"Another close call!" said Stinky.

"Let's hope they don't put us under siege, like the pigs did," said Icky.

"I was only trying to educate them," said Bryan.

Icky checked through the letterbox. "Thank God for that," he said. "They're going back down the road."

It was just as well that the dogs had retreated. Barely five minutes had passed before the sound of ice-cream chimes rang out along Spatula Drive. The tune was that well-known ancient hit, "You Were Always On My Mind", which could only mean one thing: the Brain Drain wagon.

"Do we *have* to give brains?" moaned Stinky. "I haven't got that many in the first place."

"Yes, and I really shouldn't take any chances, in case I get picked for *Superchild Head Challenge* on Channel P again," said Bryan.

"Oh, come on, you two!" said Icky. "It'll be fun! And anyway, if no one gives brains, the sewers will burst, and the whole town will be swimming in—"

"Yes, yes," said Bryan. "We get your point."

Stinky didn't get the point at all, but still followed his mates out of the front door.

"No sign of the dogs," said Icky. "That's good."

The three mates made their way to the Brain Drain wagon, which did actually look a bit like a glorified ice-cream van, except five times as big. It actually had the words NUTTY TOPPING all over the side, as a kind of joke to appeal to children, who were of course the only people left to give brains.

Two girls were waiting to greet the three mates.

29

They looked quite similar, a bit plump, with corkscrew hair and big foreheads, except one was all eager and smiley, while the other was serious and responsible.

"Hi!" said the eager one. "I'm Rosie, and this is my sister Mildred. We are your guides to giving brains."

Note from Blue Soup:

Rosie and Mildred were actually the only people on Earth who still had a job. I should have said earlier that I run everything except the Brain Drain van. The reasons for this are obvious.

Well, they are to me, anyway.

"If you'd like to step inside," said Mildred, dourly.

The three mates climbed into the van. There was a row of booths inside, each with a seat, a headset, and a touch-screen. Mildred and Rosie guided the mates to three of the booths, and instructed them to put on the headsets.

"Now!" said Rosie, brightly. "What music would you like? We recommend Easy Listening for clearing the head quickly and effectively."

"Simply make your choice from the touch screen," added Mildred.

Stinky chose 20 GOLDEN GREATS OF PERRY COMO. Icky chose ASTRO BOP FUSION TURF WAR. Bryan chose MAHLER'S SYMPHONY NUMBER 8 IN E FLAT.

"Now sit back, relax, and everything will be done for you," chirped Rosie.

Icky and Stinky had given brains several times, but it was still a strange sensation as the star-laser burned a small hole through their inner ear and began draining the grey matter within. In a way it was quite pleasant, a bit like the feeling when you go very fast over a humpback bridge, except continuously, for twenty minutes.

Mildred and Rosie had already had twenty-five customers that day. They were beginning to flag a little.

"Hot chocolate, Mil?" asked Rosie, studying the various hot drinks on offer in the van.

"Yes, please," replied Mildred. "Black, no sugar, as bitter as possible."

Rosie chose double-creamy supersickly for herself, and stabbed the on-button – or, at least, what she thought was the on-button.

"Rosie, you idiot!" yelled Mildred. "That's the drain boost!"

"Sugar!" cried Rosie, quickly stabbing it off again.

Back in the booths, the three mates had noticed nothing wrong, although Stinky did feel he'd been over a particularly high humpbacked bridge.

The machine gradually came to a standstill, and Mildred viewed the three mates with slight concern.

"I'll just conduct a short test to check your brain functions," said Mildred.

Bryan was first.

"Name?" asked Mildred.

"Bryan Brain," replied Bryan Brain.

"What colour is grass?" asked Mildred.

"Green," replied Bryan, "owing to the presence of chlorophyll, from the Greek 'khloros phullon' meaning 'green leaf'."

If Mildred was impressed, she certainly did not show it. With a little huff she turned to Icky.

"Name?" she asked.

"Icky Bats," replied Icky Bats.

"Name a bird that can't fly," asked Mildred.

"A dead 'un," replied Icky.

Tut-tut-tut, tutted Mildred, then turned to Stinky.

"Name?" she asked.

"Stinky Finger," replied Stinky Finger.

Mildred held up three fingers. "How many fingers am I holding up?" she asked.

"Er …" said Stinky.

"It's all right, Mildred," said Icky. "He didn't know that before."

Bryan and Icky returned to the House of Fun with that warm glowy feeling you get when you've done something worthy and good. Stinky, on the other hand, was quite down.

"I did know it was three," he muttered. "It just takes me time."

"It doesn't matter," said Icky.

"It does to me," said Stinky. "Sometimes I wish, just for one day, I could be brilliant."

"Forget it," said Bryan. "Everyone will hate you. Believe me, I know."

"People don't hate you cos you're brilliant," said Icky. "They hate you cos you keep telling them about it."

"I'm only being honest," replied Bryan.

Suddenly Icky caught sight of an invitation lying on the kitchen table. "We must have forgotten to post this one," he said.

Icky read over the invitation, and as he did so, scratched his head. "You know this party we're having, for Christmas?" he said.

"Yes?" said Stinky and Bryan.

"What's Christmas?" asked Icky.

The same puzzled frown came over all three housemates. Christmas? It *sounded* familiar, but … what exactly did it mean?

"It's as if … there's a gap in my head where Christmas used to be," said Stinky.

"You don't think … something went wrong with the Brain Drain?" asked Bryan.

The puzzled frowns turned to looks of alarm.

"They've sucked Christmas out of our heads!" cried Icky.

All three began pacing the room at great speed, this way and that, like ants with their nest kicked over.

"I knew we shouldn't have given brains!" cried Bryan.

"How can we have a Christmas party," cried Stinky, "when we don't know what Christmas is?"

"We've got to think!" cried Icky. "Think hard!"

The three mates sat down at the table. Icky frowned furiously. Bryan mashed his fist into his forehead. Stinky gazed at an imaginary fly buzzing from side to side.

Suddenly Bryan had a thought. "There was this guy," he said. "A big guy."

"Was it Guy Fawkes?" asked Stinky.

"No, his name was … Santa," said Bryan. "Santa … something."

"Santa Pants," said Icky.

"Santa Pants," said Bryan. "It does ring a bell."

"*I* remember Santa," said Stinky. "He rode round in a chariot of fire pulled by a snowman."

"How come the fire never melted the snowman?" said Icky.

"It was fireproof," said Stinky. "Like a sofa."

"A snowman like a sofa?" said Icky. "I can't imagine that."

"I've just remembered something else," said Bryan. "I wrote a letter to Santa once."

"Did he reply?" asked Stinky.

"No," said Bryan. "I put it on the fire and burned it."

"Why did you do that?" asked Stinky.

"Haven't a clue," said Bryan. "It seemed to make sense at the time."

Stinky, Bryan and Icky fell into deep reflective thought, like you do when you stare at a fire. Then, suddenly, Stinky came back to life. "Songs!" he said. "There were songs!"

"What kind of songs?" asked Bryan.

"Special Christmas songs!" said Stinky.

"I remember a special Christmas song!" cried Icky.

"How did it go?" asked Stinky.

Icky frowned. "I've got the tune," he said, "but not the words."

"Sing the tune," said Stinky, "then maybe the words will come."

"OK," said Icky. He began to sing, very loud, as if Stinky and Bryan were at the end of a large aircraft hangar instead of right next to him. It was a jaunty song, a singalong song, and as he sang it his arm began to pump and his foot began to stomp. Suddenly words began to tumble from his lips:

"Oh, tie a yellow doofer round your mo-ther's leg,

She's got three long ears and a pla-stic bag!

If I don't see a yellow doofer round your mother's leg,

I'll spit on the bus, jump and cuss,

Sting you like a bee!

If I don't see a yellow doofer round your mo-ther's knee!"

Icky's frantic concert ended, his shoulders slumped, and he began to look quite depressed.

"Are you *sure* that's a Christmas song, Icky?" asked Stinky gently.

"Probably not," said Icky.

Bryan studied the invitation again. "It says 'YOU WILL REMEMBER THIS FEAST FOR EVER'. That suggests there is food involved."

"Fish and chips," suggested Icky.

"No, it's a bird," said Bryan. "Definitely a bird."

"Blue tit," said Icky.

"Bigger than that," said Bryan.

"Albatross," said Icky.

"I'm sure I'd remember if it was albatross," said Bryan.

"Eagle," suggested Stinky.

"Eagle," murmured Bryan, stroking his chin thoughtfully. "That *does* ring a bell."

Stinky glowed with satisfaction.

"Or was it an emu?" said Bryan.

Stinky was determined not to lose his moment of glory. He declared that he was absolutely 101% cast-iron certain that the bird in question was an eagle. Neither Bryan nor Icky had ever seen Stinky so certain about anything. However unlikely it sounded, it had to be right.

"Good," said Bryan. "Now all we've got to do is hunt one down."

Chapter Three

The Super Safari Viewing Lounge was the three mates' favourite room in the House of Fun. They'd actually only discovered it a few days before, since from the outside it looked like a broom cupboard. In point of fact it was a wide airy room, and the wall at one end was a giant glass screen, through which they could see a fantastic landscape of Africa. Or Australia. Or Borneo. It depended on which button they pressed on the remote control.

This was the magical West Garden of the House of Fun.

As yet the three mates hadn't ventured out into the West Garden, although there was a door. Bryan had had a bad experience of the back garden (which was basically Outer Space), and they were all a bit nervous of getting lost for ever in infinite nothingness.

However, if they wanted an eagle, the West Garden was the obvious place to look.

"Where do eagles live?" asked Icky, pausing over the remote.

"High," said Stinky.

"The Scottish Highlands, actually," said Bryan.

Icky pressed a button, and there before them appeared rough craggy mountains, thin dark lakes, and endless acres of heather.

"Now we've got to attract one," said Bryan.

"You attract helicopters by putting a big H on the ground," said Icky. "Maybe we should put a big E."

Bryan sighed wearily, and Stinky, who couldn't spell "eagle", just looked confused.

"We could attract it with some prey," suggested Bryan. "A live rabbit, tied to a stick with a piece of string. Then when the eagle comes for the rabbit, we sling a net over it, then brain it with a rolling-pin."

"What, the rabbit?" said Stinky.

"The eagle, you goon!" said Bryan.

Icky had always been fond of rabbits, and the idea of tying one up as bait did not appeal to him at all. "Why don't *you* be bait, Bryan?" he suggested.

"Eagles don't eat people," said Bryan, although he didn't sound altogether sure.

There was a pause, while the three briefly pictured being Christmas lunch for a big bird, instead of the other way round.

"I can do eagle calls," said Stinky, suddenly.

"What?" said Icky. "Why didn't you say so before?"

"No one asked me," said Stinky.

Note from Blue Soup:
After the Spoonheads had taught most animals how to speak like humans, some dogs started a campaign called Save The Bark. This began to spread rapidly, and as a result the Spoonheads decided to teach some humans animal and bird calls, so as to even things up.

"I've got it!" said Icky, excitedly. "Stinky dresses up as an eagle, and pretends to be its mate!"

"Frabjous idea, Icky!" cried Stinky.

"Astral!" cried Icky.

"Gonk!" cried Stinky.

"Ducks-deluxe!" cried Icky.

Bryan, you may have noticed, was not joining in with the celebrations. "The vision of the eagle," he said, "is at least eight times as powerful as our own. Even a short-sighted eagle could tell its mate from Stinky covered in feathers."

Icky wasn't listening. He was so excited at the idea of dressing Stinky as an eagle, all reason had gone out of the window. The two of them set off for the dressing-up room, with Stinky not really sure this was a good idea, but swept along by his great pal's enthusiasm.

For once, however, the dressing-up room was a disappointment. All they could find was a comedy chicken suit and an Apache head-dress, which did at least have feathers. Stinky tried this on but felt totally stupid. Icky tried it on, didn't feel stupid at all, struck a few dramatic poses in the dressing-up mirror, then pretended to catch sight

of his own reflection and fall in love with it.

"Hmm," said Stinky. "At least you've attracted yourself."

A new idea began to dawn on Icky. It began as a rosy glow on the horizon, then flared into glorious sunshine, sending Icky in leaps and bounds around the room, nutting imaginary footballs. "That's it!" he cried.

"What's it?" said Stinky.

"The mirror!" cried Icky. "We use the mirror!"

"Hit it with the mirror!" cried Stinky.

"Er … no, Stinky," said Icky. "What I meant was, *attract* it with the mirror. So it sees its own reflection, and thinks it's another eagle!"

Stinky thought about this a while. "Do I still get to do my eagle call?" he asked.

"Of course," said Icky.

"Let's do it," said Stinky.

Icky and Stinky set about taking down the big mirror. Meanwhile, downstairs, Bryan had also been at work. He'd found himself a telescope, a few metres of fishing net, and a whacking great rolling-pin. By the time Icky and Stinky arrived with the mirror, he'd already got his telescope trained on

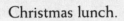

Christmas lunch.

"Enemy sighted at twelve o'clock," he said. It was something he'd heard in an old film.

"No time to lose!" cried Icky. Without bothering to explain to Bryan, Icky and Stinky lumbered the big mirror through the exit door. It was surprisingly cold and wet outside, but then again, it was the Scottish Highlands. The two great mates laid the mirror flat on a patch of heather, then retreated behind a nearby rock, where they were joined by Bryan.

"It'll never work," said Bryan.

"Why not?" said Icky.

"Because I didn't think of it," said Bryan.

At that moment, the eagle appeared directly above them. Stinky began to make soft screechy noises, a bit like an old car doing handbrake turns on a polystyrene ice rink. The eagle began zig-zagging downwards.

"Christmas lunch coming up," said Icky.

"Hmmph," said Bryan.

The plan worked like a dream. The eagle dived and landed straight on the dressing-room mirror, then just stood there, looking downwards and very confused.

"Quick!" said Bryan. "The net!"

The three mates took hold of three corners of

the fishing net, rushed out from their hidey-hole and flung it over the eagle. Then, not being sure what to do next, they all ran back again.

"Someone's got to brain it!" cried Bryan, flourishing the rolling-pin.

"You!" said Icky.

"I can't!" cried Bryan. "I've got ... a septic finger!"

"We'll draw straws," declared Icky.

Icky selected two long sprigs of heather and one short one. He arranged these in his hand with just the ends poking out.

Nervously, Bryan took his pick.

A long sprig.

Casually, Stinky did the same.

A short one.

"What does that mean again?" asked Stinky.

Bryan handed Stinky the rolling-pin. "Bring home the birdie, Stinky," said Bryan. "And don't forget the giblets."

The hour of destiny had arrived for Stinky. He took the rolling-pin, and with a deep breath headed back to where they netted the eagle. Bryan did think about watching, but Icky was already sitting with his arms clasped round his

47

ears and his hands covering his eyes. Bryan decided it would be kind of brotherly to do the same.

A minute passed. Icky thought he heard a dull CLUNK, but it might have been a large pine cone falling off a tree. Bryan thought he heard a muffled SQUEAL, but it might have been two rabbits meeting head-on in a narrow tunnel.

And then, both of them really did hear something. It was the sound of conversation, and it was getting closer.

"Salmon *is* tasty," said a very familiar voice, "but I wouldn't trust it raw."

"Take my word for it," said a less familiar voice, "the texture is out of this world."

Icky and Bryan opened their eyes. Around the corner of the rock came Stinky, chatting amiably with the eagle they had just netted.

"Icky and Bryan," said Stinky, "this is Orforix."

"Call me Orfor," said the eagle, holding out a wing.

Not knowing what else to do, Icky and Bryan gave Orfor a weak wingshake. Then all four of them stood around feeling awkward.

"Sounds like a kicking house, this house you live in," said Orfor.

"Yes," said Bryan. "Yes, it's great."

There was another awkward silence.

"Would you like to come in and have a cup of tea?" asked Stinky.

"You're a gent," replied Orfor. Without a second's hesitation he sprang towards the house, leaving Stinky to face a most unhappy Bryan.

"Stinky," said Bryan, "we're supposed to cook it, not make friends with it!"

"I couldn't help it," said Stinky. "We got talking."

"Does seem like quite a nice bloke," mumbled Icky.

"He's not a bloke," grumbled Bryan, "he's Christmas dinner."

It didn't take Orfor long to settle in. Like all eagles, he liked to keep his nest clean, and it seemed only natural to do the same for the House of Fun. He was soon clearing up the dirty clothes and feather-sweeping the dusty corners. Meanwhile Bryan was getting more and more uptight.

"This cannot carry on!" he hissed. "Someone has got to speak to him!"

"Maybe we can break it to him gently," suggested Stinky.

"What, that we're going to eat him?" said Icky. "How do you break that gently?"

Bryan leapt to his feet. "Obviously, *muggins* is going to have to do it!" he hissed. "Seeing as *muggins* is the only one who isn't too soft!"

Bryan marched out, slamming the door behind him, leaving Stinky more confused than ever. "Who's Muggins?" he asked.

"Never mind," said Icky.

Orfor was cleaning the window in the Viewing Lounge as Bryan strode in. "I need to have a word with you," said Bryan, in his best headmaster voice.

"Sure," said Orfor. "Fire away, er ... sorry, forgot your name."

"Bryan," replied Bryan. "Bryan Brain."

"Bryan, of course!" said Orfor. "Sorry about that. I'm rubbish with names. I should have remembered yours, you being brainy and that."

Bryan's brow furrowed. "How did you know I was brainy?" he asked.

Orfor laughed. "It's obvious, isn't it?" he asked.

"Is it?" said Bryan.

"You only have to *look* at you," said Orfor. "The set of your jaw. The sparkle in your eyes."

Bryan's face pinked a little. "Very observant of you," he noted.

"I'm an eagle," replied Orfor.

"Right," said Bryan, cottoning on. "You've got to be observant, to be an eagle."

"Got it in one," replied Orfor. "Not surprisingly."

By now Bryan was feeling a warm buzzy feeling, like you do when you get a round of applause. He paused for a moment and tried to remember why he'd come into the room.

"Er ..." he began. "You may have noticed the

51

roasting-tray in the kitchen—"

"Can I ask you a question?" said Orfor suddenly.

"What?" said Bryan.

"Is it unusual," asked Orfor, "for people to be very clever *and* good-looking?"

Bryan's pink face warmed up to a full-on red. "Well ..." he mumbled. "There's not *that* many of us, I suppose ..."

"Sorry," said Orfor. "I interrupted you. What were you going to say about the roasting tray?"

"Er ..." stammered Bryan. "Would you mind cleaning it?"

Chapter Four

Bryan was very clear about it. He hadn't backed down from telling Orfor. He had simply decided that it would be better to break the news when Christmas arrived. That way they could get Orfor nicely fattened up and have the house tidied into the bargain.

And anyway, they had other things to deal with. The morning post, for example. There was a pile of letters on the mat as high as Icky.

Bryan opened the first.

> Yo, dudes!
> I'll be there! Hope there's a pressie under the tree!
> Ratso

"Pressie?" said Stinky.

"Tree?" said Icky.

"Do you think it's *any* tree?" asked Stinky.

"I doubt it," said Icky. "It's bound to be a special kind of tree."

"Let's brainstorm," said Bryan. "Name some trees."

"Oak tree," said Stinky.

"Chestnut tree," said Bryan.

"Hiss-tree and Poe-tree," said Icky.

"Anyway," said Stinky, "what's a 'pressie'?"

"It's a kiss," said Icky. "You kiss under the tree."

"Eurrgh!" said Bryan.

"No, there's something else you kiss under," said Stinky. "Something ... toe."

"Big toe?" suggested Icky.

"No, not that," said Stinky.

"Little toe," said Icky.

"Little toe," repeated Stinky. "That sounds more like it. You kiss under the little toe."

"I'm not kissing under your little toe!" said Icky. "It's covered in fungus!"

"Not since the worms ate it," said Stinky.

"Forget it," said Bryan. "Let's open the next one."

Hi, Stinks and co!

Love to come to your party, mates! Hope you've got the decs up!

Arnie Bunko

"Decs?" said Stinky.

"Is that like decks on ships?" asked Icky.

"This is getting worse and worse!" said Bryan.

But it was about to get worse still. Every single letter mentioned some new and meaningless thing. Yule logs, fairy lights, Christmas puddings – there was no end to it.

"There's something here about … a red-nosed reindeer," said Icky.

"A *what*?" gasped Bryan.

"A reindeer … with a red nose," said Icky.

"That's the last straw!" said Bryan. "We cannot do this Christmas party!"

At this thought, a terrible depression came over Stinky. He knew what people would say. Stinky's done it again. Tried, and failed.

"Why don't we just go to town," he said, "and ask someone?"

"You're forgetting something, Stinky," said Icky.

"What's that?" said Stinky.

"The dogs," said Icky.

"Are they back?" asked Stinky.

"They sure are," said Icky, "and they're looking meaner than ever."

The three mates pondered taking on the dogs, but not for long. Then Bryan had another idea.

"The Cheesy Dreams Bedroom!" he cried. "Remember when I slept there, and had a weird dream, and remembered where I'd left my toothbrush?"

"Oh yeah," said Icky. "But that was probably luck, and anyway, it was only remembering one little thing."

"Yes," said Bryan, "but I only ate one little square of cheddar on a cocktail stick. If I tried the whole cheeseboard …"

"Could be risky," said Stinky.

"I'm that kind of guy," said Bryan.

This was news to Icky and Stinky, but Bryan was strangely confident, probably because he alone had spent a night in the Cheesy Dreams Bedroom (as a result of a game of dare). The others had been well impressed with him, and he'd liked that.

The Cheesy Dreams Bedroom was an unusual shape. It was very narrow, almost pointed, where the door came in – then it fanned out wide to the end where the bed was. There was no furniture in the room apart from this bed (which looked very comfy) and a matching bedside fridge.

At half past ten precisely, Bryan headed straight for this fridge.

"Hmm," he said, opening the door. "Edam … Stilton … Cheddar … oh, and a nice lump of Dorset Blue Veiny."

"You should eat the lot!" said Icky, who had followed closely in Bryan's footsteps.

"All right," said Bryan. "I will."

"Frabjous!" said Icky, though in truth he was slightly worried. Icky didn't like to see other people doing the stupid things he'd happily do himself.

Bryan took a plate out of the fridge, loaded it high with the cheeses, and began to work his way through them. Being Bryan, he couldn't bring himself to wolf them down. He ate neatly, with polite little nibbles and endless amounts of chewing. Icky's watch was showing five to midnight when Bryan finally ate his last mouthful.

Note from Blue Soup:
Actually, Icky's watch always showed five to midnight.

"I am ready," said Bryan, climbing into bed. "Turn the light off when you leave."

Icky did as he was told. Bryan settled himself down and thought nice thoughts about being back at school and top of the class, in the good old days before the Spoonheads came and took away Bryan's fans, who all happened to be teachers.

Tonight, however, sleep just would not come. Bryan turned this way and that, counted sheep, multiplied them by thirteen, and still couldn't seem to doze off. He was just thinking about knocking himself out on the bedpost when the door creaked, and a familiar voice hissed across the dark room.

"Bryan?"

It was Icky.

"What is it?" mumbled Bryan.

"The dogs have gone," whispered Icky.

"So?" said Bryan.

"Let's go into town," said Icky.

Bryan glanced at his watch. Ten past midnight.

59

What would his parents think if he went off to town at ten past midnight?

Then again, Bryan's parents were in a space zoo.

"OK," he said.

It seemed fantastically exciting, stepping out of the house in the middle of the night. The air was fresh, the sky was full of stars, and there was a distant smell of burning rose-bushes. Sure enough, the dogs had gone, and as Icky and Bryan reached the end of the road, they saw an amazing sight. All the hills around were lit with bonfires, and the town that nestled between them was alive with

coloured lights. Across the night air came a vague hubbub of excited conversation, and the sound of strangely familiar music – music with bells, and choirs, big bouncing drums and driving rock guitar.

There ahead of them was a giant poster:

TONIGHT

AT THE SUPERKIDS FUNDOME

A **CHRISTMAS SPECTACULAR**

FEATURING SANTA AND HIS REINDEER!

XMAS NUMBER ONES MEDLEY!

XMAS PANTO!

CAROL SINGING!

DECS! PRESSIES! TREES!

"Frabjous!" said Icky. "Everything we need to know, all in one place!"

"What ducks-deluxe luck!" said Bryan.

"All we've got to do," said Icky, "is find it."

Bryan yawned. "I do feel tired," he said. "Maybe I should have a little lie-down." But the pair pressed on, down stunning starlit streets full of life and action, till another sign caught their eye:

TIM and JIM's DINER
SPECIAL TONIGHT –
CHRISTMAS PUD!

"This is just too good!" said Bryan.

"Let's pig out!" said Icky.

Bryan and Icky piled into the little café behind the sign. Since the grown-ups had gone, they'd never been into a café, mainly because they'd never seen one. After all, since the Spoonheads installed Blue Soup, no one needed to work and no one used money. There was no reason to open a café, unless, of course, you thought it was fun.

Note from Blue Soup:

In fact, this is exactly what some young people did think. As we all know, however, young people often have crazes, and sudden urges, and fads, and fashions. A few days later they get fed up with the thing that seemed so exciting and move on to something new. That is exactly what happened to the kiddy diners that sprang up all over town, which explains the scene that follows.

Icky and Bryan had hardly opened the door when they were mown down by Green-Dust Laser fire. Two boys were leaping round the tables with GDL guns, in a room full of loud music, disco smoke and burst balloons. One was bald, with a wildly excited face. The other had a face like a doughnut and small bright eyes like a bird's. He wore a stripy apron round a big dumpy belly.

"Take your shots!" yelled the baldy boy.

Icky and Bryan, remembering years of practice in the playground, flung themselves to the ground in strange twisted positions. The café boys laughed like drains.

"Your go now!" yelled the doughnut boy.

Icky sat up. "We only came in for some food," he said.

The café boys looked confused for a moment, then Icky's words seemed to click.

"Right!" said the baldy boy. He flung a menu, which Bryan, to his own amazement, caught. It was the first time Bryan had caught anything, and to make things better, the café boys gave him a round of applause.

"I like this café!" said Bryan. He looked round for the best table, but discovered there was only one left standing. The rest had been built into barricades.

"Take a seat," said the doughnut boy. "But don't forget to bring it back!"

Everyone laughed. It was a rubbishy old joke but for some reason it seemed very funny.

Bryan and Icky sat down and studied the menu:

TIM AND JIM'S SPECIALS
ALL DAY – EVERY DAY
EAT AS MUCH AS YOU LIKE

64

"Astral!" said Bryan.

"Gonk!" said Icky.

They read on:

LIME JELLY
BLACKCURRANT JELLY
ORANGE JELLY
STRAWBERRY JELLY
CHRISTMAS PUD

Icky's mouth watered. "Can you have Christmas pud *and* strawberry jelly?" he asked.

The baldy boy suddenly winced. "I've got a strawberry growing out of my you-know-what," he said.

"You want to put some cream on that!" said the doughnut boy.

Everybody fell about laughing.

"I could stick a blunt pencil in it," said Icky, "but you wouldn't get the point!"

The laughs got even louder.

"What lies on its back, a hundred feet in the air?" asked the doughnut boy.

"A dead centipede!" cried the baldy boy.

The laughter was getting quite painful. Bryan was desperate to join in. "I'll have a crocodile sandwich," he cried, "and make it snappy!"

Suddenly the laughter stopped.

The atmosphere went very cold.

The café boys turned off the music.

"What did you say?" asked the baldy boy icily.

Bryan's smile quivered nervously. "A crocodile sandwich," he repeated. "And make it ... snappy."

The café boys looked at each other, then turned to Bryan with faces like death. "We don't like being ordered about," growled the doughnut boy.

"I was just making a joke!" pleaded Bryan. "A crocodile sandwich and—"

"*Don't* say it again!" snapped the baldy boy.

Bryan shut up.

Things felt very awkward.

"We'll just have the Christmas pud, please," said Icky. "No hurry, like."

The doughnut boy stared at Bryan a while, before marching out the back. The baldy boy stared a few seconds more, then followed.

The café suddenly seemed a very gloomy place. For the first time, Bryan noticed how the walls were peeling and there was rubbish in the corners of the room.

"You shouldn't have said that," said Icky.

"We'll find out what a Christmas pudding is," replied Bryan, "then go."

Time passed. Maybe a few minutes, maybe twenty. For some reason it was hard to tell. Then, at last, the baldy boy arrived with two dishes. On each dish was a pale brown dome.

"With the chef's best wishes," said the baldy boy, with an odd, twisted smile. "Enjoy."

Bryan and Icky scanned the dishes before them. They didn't seem to be very warm.

"Maybe it's a kind of ice-cream thing," said Icky.

"Or a butterscotch milk jelly," suggested Bryan.

Bryan took a knife and prodded his pudding. "Feels more like dumpling," he said. He pushed the knife a little harder, till it popped through the outer layer.

"Hang on," he said. "There's something different inside."

Bryan pulled out the knife, and was just about to attack the pudding with his spoon, when something very disturbing occurred.

A thin, shiny black leg appeared from the pudding.

"W-what's that?" stammered Bryan.

The pudding seemed to vibrate. The crack began to open. Then the whole thing exploded, and there before the two mates was a mass of scurrying, scrabbling cockroaches. The vile insects fled the dish in a horrible, glinting, manic river, and the only thing that moved faster was Bryan. He was back on the street before his feet touched the ground. By the time Icky caught up with him, Bryan was in another area of town altogether.

"Told you not to wind those boys up!" said Icky.

"Can't be ..." gasped Bryan. "Can't be ..."

"Can't be what?" said Icky.

"Can't be a real Christmas pudding!" gasped Bryan. "Can it?"

"How do I know?" said Icky.

"Where are we, anyway?" asked Bryan.

Icky and Bryan looked around. They were on a moss-green lawn, under a sky which had somehow become quite unreal, with white clouds scudding across, even though it was the middle of the night. To one side of them was a building like a giant greenhouse, lit by a milky light. As they moved closer, the housemates realised that this building was filled with people, most of them sitting at tables and all of them completely still.

"But there's ... grown-ups," muttered Icky.

A chill went through Bryan. Something wasn't right. Then one of the people, a young boy, moved away from the others, drifted up to the side, placed his hands against the glass, and stared straight at Bryan. Bryan's heart almost stopped.

"That's ... Stig Senna," he gasped.

Icky said nothing.

"Stig Senna!" repeated Bryan. "Remember, from school?"

Icky still said nothing. Bryan turned to him. "It is Stig, isn't it?" he asked.

"Bryan," said Icky, "Stig Senna died four years ago."

Bryan stared at Icky in horror. "I'm getting out of here!" he cried. With that, he turned on his heel and ran – faster and faster, faster and faster, till he was out of town altogether and down at the bay. He didn't stop till he was on the spit of sand that went out from the headland, where he paused for breath and waited for Icky to catch up. But just as he began to feel safe, he noticed how the black sea-water had rushed in behind them, cutting them off from the land. Suddenly realising the intense danger, he began to make his way back. Too late! The waters were already up to his middle, and rising fast. There was no way he could escape.

And then it dawned on him. "Icky!" he cried. "Is this a dream?"

"Wake up then!" cried Icky.

"I can't!" cried Bryan.

"Force open your eyes!" cried Icky.

Bryan fought and fought to open his eyes, but it was as if there were iron weights holding them down.

With a huge, superhuman effort he finally tore them open and sat bolt upright, panting for breath.

To his surprise, Bryan found he was on a park bench, still on the road into town. Icky was beside him.

"Why aren't I in bed?" he asked.

"Have you forgotten?" said Icky. "We were going into town."

"I thought that was a dream," said Bryan.

"No, that was real," said Icky. "You got tired and had a lie-down. That was probably when your dream started."

"Ah," said Bryan.

"Get a move on," said Icky. "We'll miss the Christmas Spectacular at the Superkids Fundome."

"The Christmas Spectacular?" said Bryan. "That wasn't part of the dream?"

"No, don't you remember?" said Icky. "We saw the poster just before you had your lie-down."

"Right," said Bryan. "What about Tim and Jim's Diner?"

"What's Tim and Jim's Diner?" asked Icky.

"Right," said Bryan. "That was a dream."

"Guess so," said Icky.

Bryan got up, opened his eyes very wide just to make sure they were open, then joined Icky on the road to town.

Note from Blue Soup:

This really is a very long chapter. I don't really like to have chapters this long, but things just keep happening. I therefore propose that we have a short break now, although there is no break in the story. Perhaps you could get out your nice crayons and do a picture of Bryan and Icky on their journey to town. Maybe you could send the best ones to me, then I could digest them all and produce something rather better than your efforts.

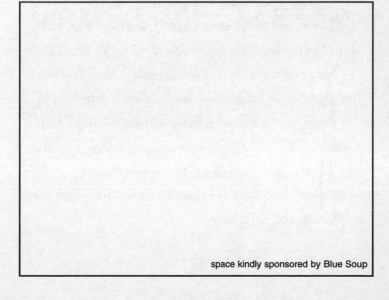

space kindly sponsored by Blue Soup

"I wonder where this Superkids Fundome is?" asked Bryan.

"I thought you knew everything," said Icky.

"Not everything," said Bryan. "Just most things."

As he said these words, Bryan had a strange and uncomfortable feeling. Something was missing. Something very crucial.

"Icky," he said nervously. "Could you look down and tell me something?"

"What's that?" asked Icky.

"Have I … got any trousers on?" asked Bryan.

Icky looked. "No," he replied.

Panic gripped Bryan. "Are you sure?" he gasped.

"Certain," replied Icky. "In fact, you've got nothing on at all."

Bryan folded up in a hopeless attempt to cover himself. This was the worst thing to happen to him since coming second in the school geography test.

"H-how did that happen?" he gasped.

"I meant to say something," said Icky, "but you seemed quite happy."

"I've got to get cover!" squealed Bryan.

He weaved this way and that, desperate for a corner to hide in. There were none. Icky faded into the distance as Bryan sprinted for an open door further up the road. With huge relief he got inside, into a dark corridor, where no one could see him. Up ahead was another door – maybe the door to a room with trousers in it, thought Bryan. He hurried on, seized the handle, and flung it open.

Immediately he was hit by a blast of light. Noise welled up all around him – huge, awesome laughter, so loud it could have been the laughter of giants.

Bryan's eyes cleared. He was standing on a stage, in a huge, dome-shaped arena, with a hundred thousand braying kids pointing straight at him.

"No-o-o-o-o-o!" screamed Bryan. With that, he woke up, in bed, staring at the door of the Cheesy Dreams Bedroom.

Icky and Stinky burst in.

"You all right, Bryan?" asked Stinky.

Bryan fought for breath. "Bad dream," he gasped.

"Was it like your dream about **Satan's crypt**?" asked Icky.

"Worse," replied Bryan.

"What did you remember about Christmas?" asked Icky.

Bryan thought back over his nightmare. "Er ... nothing," he said.

"Maybe you should eat some more cheese," suggested Icky.

"No!" squealed Bryan. "No more cheese!"

Stinky sighed. "Ah well," he said. "Back to square one."

Chapter Five

"We could try the tennis ball gown game," suggested Bryan.

Five more days had passed and the mates were getting desperate.

"What's the tennis ball gown game?" asked Stinky.

"I say a word, and you say the first word that comes into your head," said Bryan. "It might spark off a memory."

"What if no word at all comes into my head?" asked Stinky, who feared this was more than likely.

"We'll cross that bridge when we come to it," said Bryan.

"Now you're *really* confusing me," said Stinky.

Bryan sorted through the party replies, which Orfor had tidied into a neat pile.

"Right," he said. "We'll start with … pudding."

Stinky thought for a few moments. "Bowl," he replied, much relieved.

"Haircut," said Icky.

"What did you say that for?" asked Bryan.

"I don't know!" said Icky. "You told me to say the first word that came into my head!"

"Maybe there's something in it," said Stinky.

"Maybe there's hair in a Christmas pudding," suggested Icky.

"What, hair off your head?" asked Bryan. "Or hare like a rabbit?"

"How can you have hair like a rabbit?" asked Stinky. "A rabbit's got fur."

Bryan banged his head gently against the wall. "This is going nowhere," he said.

"We need to find that brain donor van," said Icky, "and get our brains back!"

Bryan stopped banging his head and gave a weary sigh. "But Icky," he said, "the brain donor van could be in Timbuctu by now."

"We'll go there then!" said Icky.

"What I meant," said Bryan huffily, "is that we haven't got a clue where it is."

There was a short silence, then Stinky piped up, "We could look on the card."

"What card?" asked Bryan.

"The one that came through the door," said Stinky. "It's got a list of places on the other side. The places the van is going."

"*What?*" said Bryan. "Why didn't you say?"

"No one asked," replied Stinky.

Bryan briefly thought about throttling Stinky, till he remembered that Stinky was at least twice as strong as he was. He settled for racing pell-mell to the front door, with the others in hot pursuit.

The card was still on the mat. Bryan picked it up and turned it over:

THE BRAIN DRAIN WILL BE IN THE FOLLOWING AREAS OVER THE NEXT FORTNIGHT:

13 Dec: Chestnut Crescent

14 Dec: Victoria Grove

15 Dec: Cherry Blossom Drive

16–31 Dec: The Planet Honk

"The Planet Honk?" said Icky. "Where the bleep is that?"

"It's the nearest planet to Earth," replied Bryan.

"Nearest planet to Earth?" said Icky. "I thought that was Mars."

"Venus, actually," said Bryan, "till the Spoonheads dragged Honk into the solar system."

"Why did they do that?" asked Icky.

"They wanted more shade," replied Bryan.

"I wondered what that big green disc was," said Stinky.

"The problem is," said Bryan, "how do we get there?"

The three mates pondered a while.

"I suppose," said Icky, "we go out the back door."

Bryan shivered at the thought of this. He had been the first one to discover that the back garden consisted of Outer Space, and wasn't keen to make another visit.

"Do you think there's some kind of space module somewhere?" asked Stinky.

"I'd have thought so," said Icky. "Your Uncle Nero thought of everything."

"We could ask him," suggested Stinky. "When

does he wake up next?"

Icky checked his glow-in-the-dark date strap. "Forty-nine years," he replied.

"Is that after Christmas?" asked Stinky.

"It's after forty-nine Christmases," replied Icky.

"That's no good then," said Stinky.

Suddenly there was a squawk from the kitchen. "Could you guys help me?"

"It's Orfor," said Stinky.

"Maybe he's been trying to clean the oven again," said Icky, "and got stuck."

"Quick!" said Bryan. "Let's switch it on!"

The three mates hurried to the kitchen, but to Bryan's disappointment, Orfor was nowhere near the oven.

"It's this dishwasher," said Orfor. "I can't seem to get it to work."

None of the three mates had ever been near the dishwasher, since they only ate off paper plates. In fact, they didn't even know it *was* a dishwasher. As far as they were concerned, it was just a big brass thing that stood in the corner of the kitchen and was good to bounce balls off.

"I could give it a kick," suggested Stinky.

"We don't want to break the cups and saucers," said Orfor.

"I know," said Icky, "I'll get inside."

Icky, as you may know, was a fairly small person, and never missed an opportunity to climb into things. There was very little chance this would help to repair the dishwasher, but it would probably make for an amusing adventure.

"Easy as you go, Icky," said Stinky, helping his best mate through the dishwasher door.

"If I'm not back in five minutes," said Icky, "I've probably gone through to a magic kingdom."

Stinky shuddered at the thought. He still

remembered the time he and Icky had been messing about in a wardrobe and found themselves in a snow-covered forest with four posh kids and a lion that thought it was God.

Or was that a book he'd read?

"See anything yet, Icky?" called Bryan.

"Sure have!" came a muffled cry.

A few clanks and rattles came from inside the dishwasher, then Icky reappeared, holding a casserole dish and a space helmet.

"I think we've found the module," he said.

Bryan held out his hand and Stinky studied the three straws. "I can't be unlucky *twice* in the same week," he remarked. With that, he pulled out his chosen straw, which, to be honest, did not look very long.

"Tough luck, Stinky," said Bryan, opening his hand to show two very much longer straws.

Stinky's shoulders sagged. "It's a shame the capsule won't take two," he said. "It's going to be very lonely."

"Look on the bright side, Stinky," said Bryan. "You'll be the one who gets his brains back."

"*If* I find the van," sighed Stinky.

"You'll do it, Stinks," said Icky. "Here's your going-away present." He handed Stinky a can of Cool Spring Forest underarm spray.

"Underarm spray?" said Stinky. "What's that for?"

Icky tried to think of a nice way of putting it. "Thing is, Stinky," he said, "you stink. *We* don't mind, but the people on Planet Honk might."

"Oh," said Stinky. "I see." He studied the can, then put it in his inside pocket, but only to be polite. He didn't have any plans to use it.

"And you'd better take these," said Bryan, handing Stinky two AA batteries. "You don't want to be running out of fuel."

"Good thinking, Bryan," said Stinky. He took the batteries, put on his helmet, checked he'd got his Ordnance Survey map of Planet Honk, and climbed into the space capsule. Then he solemnly gave the parting speech he'd spent all night planning, except no one could hear him through the space helmet. Icky shut the capsule door, Bryan opened the back door, and with a whirr and a hum, Stinky made a rapid exit from planet Earth.

Chapter Six

The space module didn't go so badly, considering it hadn't been used for about fifteen years. It even had a little radio, which picked up all of the space-pirate radio stations. Stinky got to know all the latest galactic hits and also which spaceways to avoid because of comets causing long tailbacks. The radio was doubly useful because the Auto-search function not only found the radio stations, but also steered the craft to the nearest planet, which, as you know, was Honk.

And so it was that Stinky Finger became the ten thousand and third person to land on Earth's nearest planet.

Note from Blue Soup:

Honk was uninhabited when the Spoonheads first dragged it into the solar system. They organised a competition called "Win the Holiday Of a Lifetime!", and the ten thousand lucky winners were sent off to form a colony. The Spoonheads originally intended to create a Theme Planet to go alongside their space zoo, but (as I am sick of telling you by now) got called away unexpectedly. The ten thousand lucky winners were left with five thousand shovels, a few cranes, and a half-built Alligator Crater Log Ride. Unlike Earth, there was no Blue Soup to sort out all the problems, and no one was exactly sure how the ten thousand kids were getting on – which was one of the reasons why the Brain Drain had been sent there.

The door to the space module opened. A cloud of moths, dust and greenish gas flew out, followed by Stinky.

Stinky immediately found himself surrounded by a gang of suspicious-looking kids in dirty work clothes, carrying shovels.

"Where are you from?" barked a red-eyed girl

with blonde hair and sticky-out ears.

"Earth, of course," replied Stinky.

"Who sent you?" squealed a weedy little lad with a face like a rat.

"Er ..." said Stinky.

"Was it Lardy McFardy?" rasped the red-eyed girl.

"Who's Lardy McFardy?" asked Stinky.

"You know Lardy McFardy!" squealed the rat-faced boy. "Lardy McFardy, the King of the Moon!"

"Never heard of him," replied Stinky.

"Yes, you have!" spat the red-eyed girl. "He's on Earth right now, recruiting an army to attack us!"

Stinky thought very hard. He was often the last person to know about things, and it was just possible he'd missed this Lardy McFardy, especially after living indoors for nine months. But he really couldn't remember Bryan saying anything about him, and Bryan would surely know.

"Who told you about this Lardy McFardy?" he asked.

"The king!" cried the rat-faced boy.

"What king?" asked Stinky.

"King Dung!" they all cried. "Almighty Ruler of the Land of the Lingering Ming!"

"Land of the Lingering Ming?" repeated Stinky. "Where's that?"

"Here!" they all cried.

"Oh," said Stinky. "Sorry. I thought I was on Planet Honk."

Suddenly the red-eyed girl thrust her shovel towards Stinky. "That's what Lardy McFardy calls it!" she cried.

"I've never heard of Lardy McFardy!" pleaded Stinky. "I just came here to find the Brain Drain!"

"Seize him!" came a great cry. The whole gang descended as one on Stinky, fixing him in a vice-like grip.

"Have I said the wrong thing?" asked Stinky.

"Throw him in prison!" squealed the rat-faced boy.

A boy and a girl took an arm each and began to frogmarch Stinky away from the space capsule. The boy, a thick-set lad with a mop of greasy black curls, seemed particularly interested in Stinky's smell. Several times he took a sniff of him, recoiled in horror, then took a sniff again. But Stinky was only vaguely aware of the boy. He was more concerned with where he was being taken, and if he would ever see his great mates again.

Planet Honk was a dire place. It was like one huge council rubbish tip, with people digging trenches everywhere and nothing growing except some pale and withered Brussels sprouts. A few kids were harvesting these sprouts, looking very depressed. Everyone seemed anxious. No one smiled.

A little settlement came into view. There were a few old caravans and a couple of rows of portakabins. Stinky was led into one of the caravans, which was empty apart from a bed made from cardboard boxes.

"First we will teach you to love King Dung," said the red-eyed girl. "Then we'll probably torture you a bit."

"Nothing personal," said the greasy-hair boy. "We just want to find out what you know."

"I don't know anything!" pleaded Stinky. "That's why I'm looking for the Brain Drain!"

"We'll soon see about that!" snarled the greasy-hair boy. With that, he slammed the caravan door, leaving Stinky with nothing but mild terror and terrible homesickness.

The kids of Planet Honk obviously wanted Stinky to sweat a bit. They weren't back for at least two hours, by which time it was night, which was a kind of dirty brown colour.

Each kid held a large vase-type thing with a stopper in it.

"W-what are they?" muttered Stinky nervously.

"The greatest aromas of King Dung," replied the red-eyed girl, "bottled for the generations of the future."

"You must sample them all!" ordered the rat-faced boy.

"Is this the torture?" asked Stinky.

"No," replied the greasy-hair boy. "This is the good bit."

Stinky was led down the line of vases. There was King Dung's Evening Armpit Stench, 10th February ... King Dung's Rubbery Bottom Aroma, 5th April ... King Dung's Fungus-Ridden Toe Odour, 25th August ... and King Dung's Fly-Blown Cheese Breath, 1st October.

None of it, frankly, impressed Stinky very much.

"When do we get to the *really* bad smells?" he asked.

"Impudent oaf!" squealed the rat-faced boy. He didn't actually know what *impudent* meant, but he'd heard it in a film once.

"Torture him!" cried the red-eyed girl.

"Leave that to me," snarled the greasy-hair boy, rubbing his hands together gleefully.

"We want to join in!" cried all the others.

"No," said the greasy-hair boy. "There is a special place for people like this, with special things in it. Most of you must never know where it is, by order of King Dung."

The rest of the kids seemed disappointed, but (unfortunately for Stinky) the greasy-hair boy seemed to know what he was doing. He was also very strong, as Stinky found out as he was tied up and frogmarched away from the caravan. Only one other boy went with them, a strange freckly lad with an oo-ar country accent. But not much was said as they tramped further and further away from the settlement, into a more and more miserable landscape.

The three eventually reached an old concrete bunker in the midst of a field of thorns. Stinky was bundled inside. To his surprise, four more kids were playing a game of table-baseball in there. They looked up at Stinky like startled cats, then calmed down as they saw the others.

"It's OK," barked the greasy-hair boy. "He's friendly."

"Eh?" said Stinky.

"Untie him, Dibs," ordered the greasy-hair boy.

To his amazement, Stinky's hands were freed and he was offered a box to sit on and a cup of warm tea.

"Er ..." he said, "... is this the torture?"

The greasy-hair boy sniffed. "What's your name, pal?" he asked.

"Stinky," replied Stinky. "Stinky Finger."

"Welcome, Stinky," said the greasy-hair boy, shaking Stinky's hand. "I'm Sooty McCrum. This is Dibs ... Weevil ... Tinky-Winky ... Ems ... and Susan."

"We're the Resistance," they chorused.

"Ah," said Stinky, nodding thoughtfully. "Is that the resistance to King Dung, or the resistance to Lardy McFardy?"

The room was filled with sounds of disgust.

"Lardy McFardy don't exist!" sneered Dibs.

Stinky was pleased to hear this. "I *knew* I hadn't heard of him," he said.

Sooty McCrum took up a seat close opposite to Stinky and looked him in the eyes. "Let me put you in the picture," he said.

"Please do," said Stinky.

"The so-called Land of the Lingering Ming," said Sooty, "is in a mess."

"I can see that," said Stinky.

"King Dung's in trouble," explained Sooty.

94

"It is only the power of his stink which keeps him in power. And without sprouts, he'll hardly smell at all."

Ems, a tall, clever-looking girl, took over. "The sprout harvest is failing," she explained. "To get the Brussels he needs, Dung needs to invade Earth."

"Invade Earth?" gasped Stinky. "But I thought the others said Earth was going to invade Honk?"

"That's what Dung wants them to believe," said Sooty. "He wants them to live in fear of Earth and hate Earth people. Then he'll persuade them to attack Earth before Earth attacks us."

"Hmm," said Stinky. "He sounds like a very clever man."

"Man?" scoffed Sooty. "He's just a boy! He only became king because he killed Matty Snick."

"Matty Snick was the hardest boy on the planet," explained Ems. "One day he picked a fight with Dung. Dung managed to get his toe up Matty's nose and the fumes finished him off. After that, everyone was scared of Dung. They thought his smell had mystic powers."

"The time has come to rid ourselves of Dung for good," said Sooty. "And that's where you come in."

A feeling of dread welled up in Stinky. "Me?" he said. "What can I do?"

"Isn't it obvious?" said Ems.

"Not to me," said Stinky.

"Dung makes out he's the smelliest person in the universe," said Sooty. "But now we know he isn't. You are."

"We're going to storm the palace," said Ems, "and crown you the new king."

"You'll either be a hero," added Sooty, "or die in a blaze of glory."

Stinky shuddered. He'd never had plans to die in a blaze of glory. He was quite happy to live in a faint smoulder of ordinariness. "Why don't you just do without a king?" he suggested.

"The others won't stand for it," replied Ems.

"It is your Destiny," added Sooty.

Stinky had no idea what to say, mainly because he didn't know what Destiny was. "But ... I only came here to find the Brain Drain," he mumbled.

"Then come with us," said Sooty, "because the Brain Drain is locked up in King Dung's palace."

"How do you know?" asked Stinky.

"Dibs used to work for the king," replied Sooty.

"He only came over to us last week."

The freckly oo-ar boy gave a crooked little smile. "Long live King Stinky!" he cried.

"Long live King Stinky!" cried the rest of the Resistance.

"Does this mean you're not going to torture me?" asked Stinky.

Chapter Seven

The Resistance set off in the dead of night, which was even browner than the start of it. Dibs assured them that Dung's guards were asleep at that time, and if they could knock out the automatic alarms, they could reach the king without any trouble. All of the Resistance were very determined, and everyone knew their job. It almost made Stinky feel confident, till he saw what they had to get in to. This was the famous Alligator Crater Log Ride, which King Dung had turned into his palace. There was a high wire fence, and inside that a snaking canal which disappeared into a black hole in a giant fake mountain. Stinky always stuck to the dodgems when he went to the fair, and he didn't like the look of this ride one bit.

"All set, folks?" said Ems, who seemed to be in charge now.

The Resistance nodded, and checked their slingshots and shovel-ends.

"Let's go," said Ems.

Dibs went to work on a lock on the gate into the compound. It was a simple combination, and posed no problem at all. The Resistance slipped silently inside and began filing on to the floating logs. Stinky took his place at the back,

Sooty released the log-gate, and the logs set off down the dark, choppy waters.

Soon they were making stomach-churning turns and dips, but no one yelled and no one screamed. Everyone had their eyes fixed on that hole in the mountain, and as they entered it, the Resistance took hold of their weapons and readied themselves for the big moment.

Behind them there was a creak, and a metal grille came down.

"Is that supposed to happen?" asked Ems.

Dibs didn't answer.

The lights went out.

"What's going on?" said Sooty.

The logs were slowing to a halt. Besides them was a landing platform. And the landing platform was not empty.

"Get back!" yelled Ems. "Get back, everybody!"

Too late. The Resistance were surrounded. King Dung's private army was everywhere. A blinding spotlight cut through the gloom, and after a hopeless struggle, all but one of the Resistance were captured.

"Well done, Dibs," said a deep voice.

Dibs took his place amongst the army, getting back-pats and handshakes by the dozen. "So long, comrades," he sneered at the Resistance. "Enjoy the king's prison!"

The Resistance were dragged off one by one, till only Stinky was left.

"That's him," said Dibs.

"We thought so," said the guards, shielding their noses from Stinky's rare and special aroma.

Stinky was getting quite used to being frog-marched around by now. But the king's guards were particularly rough. They took him down a corridor and pushed him through a pair of giant green doors. Stinky found himself in a great underground cavern, full of control-panels, busy people, and the most bog-awful smell. To the left, on a kind of stage, was the Brain Drain van. To the right was a cage, hanging over a crater full of alligators. Inside the cage were Mildred and Rosie, the Brain Drain girls. Straight in front of Stinky was the back of a luxurious chair, the colour of catsick. A crown could be seen over the top of it. The chair began to turn, slowly, revealing a dumpy, spotty-faced boy rolling a Brussels sprout calmly between his fingers.

"Mr Finger," said King Dung. "I've heard so much about you."

"You have?" said Stinky.

"Please," said King Dung. "Come a little closer."

Stinky edged forward. King Dung took a deep breath, then quickly held up his hand. "That's close enough, thank you," he said. He chewed thoughtfully on the sprout. "Well, Mr Finger," he said. "I'm afraid you're going to have to die."

"I thought so," said Stinky. It had been that kind of a day.

King Dung struggled to his feet. He was several inches shorter than Stinky, who wasn't particularly tall himself. "The alligator," he said, "is a creature with a most stupendous appetite. And my beauties have a particular appetite for traitors."

"The Brain Drain girls aren't traitors," said Stinky.

"Maybe not," said King Dung. "But without them, the Brain Drain is useless. And without the Brain Drain, Blue Soup will also be useless. The Earth will fall into chaos, and the sprouts will be mine for the taking."

There was a pause.

"I usually do a manic laugh at this point," said King Dung, "but I've got a sore throat today."

"Would you like a Strepsil?" offered Stinky.

"No thanks," said King Dung. "I'll just get on with killing you." With that, he pulled a laser-guided stinkhorn fungus from his pocket. "I shall take great pleasure in personally delivering you to your doom," he purred.

As King Dung advanced towards him, Stinky gave a deep sigh. He hated responsibility, but responsibilities kept arriving. Right now, the whole future of life on Earth depended on him. That meant, at the very least, he'd have to make a fight of it.

What would Icky do? Stinky asked himself.

Suddenly, Stinky had a great idea. He whipped the underarm spray from his pocket and gave the king both barrels.

"No!" cried King Dung, cowering away, "Not Fresh Ocean Mist!"

Stinky gave the can a puzzled look. "That's funny," he said. "I thought it was Cool Spring Forest."

"Get him, guards!" cried King Dung.

Stinky didn't panic. He calmly removed the crown from Dung's head and placed it on his own. "I am the stinkiest now," he said, "and I think that means you serve me."

The guards stopped still. Their senses told them Stinky was right.

"Better throw the old king in prison," said Stinky, "and release the girls."

The guards immediately obeyed. Stinky slumped on to King Dung's throne and took a deep breath. He'd never ordered people about like that before, and it was quite exhausting.

Chapter Eight

"If you can just fix on the headphones," said Mildred dourly, "we'll put the machine into reverse."

Stinky did as he was told. It felt good to be back in an old familiar place like the Brain Drain van. But after the last time, he wasn't quite so trusting in Mildred and Rosie. "You reckon this is safe?" he asked.

"Of course," said Mildred, "although we've never actually done it before."

"Are you *sure* you want to go back to Earth?" asked Rosie, brightly. "They seem to like you so much here!"

"I can't let Icky down," said Stinky. "Or Bryan," he mumbled.

"That was a *great* speech you made," said Rosie.

"It almost made me cry when you took off your crown and said that from now on, everybody on Honk was a king."

"Yes," added Mildred. "They all stink as much as each other. Can we get on with it now?"

Rosie and Mildred got to work on returning Stinky's brains. It felt a bit like the first time, except Stinky was going backwards over the hump-backed bridges. He couldn't actually hear Rosie and Mildred, but they did seem to be arguing, which worried him a bit. Several times Rosie went to switch the machine off, and several times Mildred stopped her. It seemed to be ages before the transfer was over.

"Good," said Mildred. "How do you feel?"

Stinky thought about this. "Like I want to sneeze," he said.

"That's not right," said Rosie.

"Nonsense," said Mildred. "Perfectly normal." She held up three fingers. "How many fingers?" she asked.

"Three," replied Stinky, "which is 'trois' in French and 'tre' in Italian. Of course, the source of all these languages is Latin."

"I told you, Mildred!" cried Rosie. "You were reading the dial wrong! You've gone and given him ten brains!"

Back on Earth, it was a cold, clear morning known as Christmas morning. All over town, boys and girls were making their way towards the House of Fun for THE BEST CHRISTMAS PARTY EVER. Meanwhile Icky and Bryan were going loony ape mental.

"We've got nothing!" cried Bryan. "No decs, no pressies, no tree – nothing!"

"We haven't even put the bird in the oven!" cried Icky.

"What the bleep has happened to Stinky?" wailed Bryan.

Suddenly there was an almighty CRASH. Bryan and Icky rushed to the kitchen. The back door was in splinters and the space module lay upside-down on the kitchen floor.

"I told you that cat flap wasn't big enough!" cried Bryan.

"Stinky!" cried Icky, heaving the space module on to its side, "are you all right in there?"

There was a pause, then the door to the module creaked open and Stinky crawled out.

"Must have set the co-ordinates wrong," he said.

Icky's mouth dropped open. "What did you say?" he asked.

"The co-ordinates," replied Stinky. "I must have set them wrong. Either that or there's a defect in the primary brake drive."

"W-what's happened to you?" stammered Icky.

"Apparently," said Stinky, "I've got ten brains."

"Ten brains?" gasped Icky. "What does that feel like?"

"It feels good," replied Stinky, "except I keep wanting to sneeze."

Bryan looked doubtful. "So," he said. "What do you know about Christmas?"

Stinky pressed the ends of his fingers together and nodded thoughtfully. "That depends what you mean by 'Christmas'," he replied.

"Well, *obviously*," said Bryan.

"The origins of Christmas lie in a number of ancient winter feasts," pronounced Stinky. "The earliest was Zagmuk, invented by the people of Mesopotamia. Then there was the Roman feast of Saturnalia. Yule, celebrated in Scandanavia."

There was a short pause.

"I knew that," said Bryan.

"Tell us about the tree!" said Icky.

"I shall come on to that shortly," replied Stinky. He began to pace the kitchen very slowly, hands behind his back, head in the air. "These early festivals," he continued, "celebrated the end of darkness and the return of the light. It was only in 350AD that the Bishop of Rome declared that December 25 was Christ's birthday."

"Stinky," said Icky, "the guests will be here any second."

"Very well," said Stinky. "I shall jump forward to

the sixteenth century. This was when fir trees were first brought indoors at Christmas time."

"*Fur* tree?" said Icky. "Where do we get a *fur* tree from?"

"The modern idea of Santa, on the other hand," said Stinky, "began in a poem of 1822. Many of our Christmas traditions date from the nineteenth century. The Christmas turkey, for example, was made popular by the stories of Dickens."

Icky's face dropped. "Turkey?" he said. "Not eagle?"

"We're done for!" cried Bryan.

There was a knock at the door.

"The guests!" cried Icky.

"What shall we do?" cried Bryan.

"Panic!" cried Icky.

Bryan rattled furiously at the oven door, yanked it open, and pulled out a roasting tin. "If nothing else," he said, "we've got to give them the bird."

"Orfor's not a turkey!" said Icky.

"They don't know that!" said Bryan.

"How are we going to do him in?" asked Icky.

Icky and Bryan looked to Stinky. "Go on, Stinky," said Bryan. "You're the one with *ten brains*."

Stinky pondered for a moment. "When a bird is caught by a cat," he declared, "it will sometimes die of fear."

"That's it!" said Icky. "We'll scare it to death."

"Oh yeah?" said Bryan. "How?"

Icky and Stinky's eyes met. The same idea arrived, at exactly the same time, in both of their heads.

"**Satan's Crypt**!" they cried.

There was a clap of thunder, a crack of lightning, and the whole house seemed to shake.

"If we open that door," warned Bryan, "anything could come out."

The three housemates shivered at the thought of a cloud of bats, wasps, flying spiders and poison moths, bursting out from behind that deadly door. Then they called for Orfor.

Orfor arrived, with a can of polish and a yellow duster.

"We were wondering, Orfor," said Bryan, "if you could do us a small favour."

"No sooner said than done," replied Orfor.

"The cellar needs tidying," said Icky.

"Hmm," said Orfor. "Is there an electric supply down there? I'll probably need to use the Hoover."

"Why don't you go down and check?" asked Bryan.

"OK," said Orfor.

With a skip and a whistle, Orfor set off for the cellar of certain doom. The three mates followed fearfully behind. As they arrived in the hall, they heard an awesome hammering at the front door. It sounded like half the town was out there.

"Shall I get that?" asked Orfor.

"No!" blurted Bryan.

"It's just carol singers!" said Stinky.

"Yeah!" said Icky. "It's carol singers, whatever they are!"

Orfor shrugged, placed his scaly claw on the deadly doorhandle, and turned.

The door to **Satan's Crypt** opened with an ancient creak.

A dank old rotten smell wafted up from the depths.

Nothing could be seen except a stone staircase disappearing into the dark.

"Are you sure it's safe down there?" asked Orfor.

"Bye!" said Bryan. He gave Orfor a little push and quickly shut the door.

The soft scratch of claws on steps grew quieter and quieter.

The three housemates began to feel a little guilty.

"It was your idea, Stinky," said Bryan.

"And Icky's," said Stinky.

"Bryan got out the roasting tin," said Icky.

Suddenly there was a muffled cry. Icky gulped. "Satan's got him!" he cried.

The three housemates listened hard at the door, hearts pounding. The voice of Orfor rose from the depths: "It's ... it's ... it's ... *frabjous!*" he cried.

"Eh?" said Bryan.

"*Astral!*" cried Orfor.

Icky opened the door. "Orfor?" he called. "Are you still ... alive?"

"You've just got to come down here!" cried Orfor. "It's *gonk!*"

Icky started for the steps, but Stinky held him back. Stinky's ten brains were working fast. "Wait, Icky!" he said. "What if it's Satan, speaking in the voice of Orfor?"

"Then I'll deck him!" said Icky. As usual, when Icky got excited, nothing would hold him back. He broke away from Stinky and clattered down the steps.

There was a moment's silence, then Icky's voice cried out from below: "It's ... it's ... *ducks deluxe!*"

Stinky and Bryan looked at each other. "Could be Satan, speaking in the voice of Icky," said Bryan.

"Only one way to find out," said Stinky.

Stinky and Bryan set off cautiously down the steps. Bryan had never been that friendly a person, so Stinky was surprised to find his housemate's clammy hand firmly gripping his arm. At the bottom of the steps they could see a bright light, growing brighter and brighter the closer they got.

"The electrics are working then," said Stinky.

"Satan doesn't need electrics," replied Bryan.

Stinky and Bryan reached the bottom of the steps. Slowly their eyes adjusted to the light. Icky and Orfor were standing right in front of them, arm in wing, beaming, with balloons tied to their heads. Behind them was the most stupendous barn of a room, decorated from top to bottom in coloured lights, with a mighty Christmas tree in the corner,

and a feast of snacks, chocolates, puddings and cakes laid out on star-spangled tables. There was even a fireplace, out of which was spilling a mass of presents, covered in golden paper and royal-purple ribbons and bows.

"This is what I'm looking forward to," said Orfor, lifting a huge tin which said XMAS FRABJOUS NUT ROAST SENSATION.

"But … I don't understand," said Bryan.

Stinky put his ten brains to work. It was a mighty effort, and several times he seemed about to sneeze, but at last he had the solution. "We read it wrong," he said.

"Eh?" said Bryan.

"The Book of the House of Fun," said Stinky. "We read it wrong."

"How's that?" said Icky.

"It never said **Satan's Crypt** at all," said Stinky. "It said *Santa's* Crypt!"

"Of course!" said Bryan.

"Of course!" said Orfor.

"Who's Santa again?" said Icky.

Stinky did not reply. That huge sneeze, the one he'd held back all day, was finally about to break free.

"Aa …" he said. "Aa … aa … aa …"

"CHOOOOOOOOOO!"

With that, Stinky erupted. It was the biggest sneeze ever heard in the history of the universe – a fifty-megaton face-bomb. Icky, Bryan and Orfor were sent tumbling. Stinky staggered about like an old drunk, reeling from the shock of the almighty blast. Then Icky caught sight of him, and nearly died. *"What's that coming out of your nose?"* he squealed.

"Eurrgh!" said Bryan.

"Eurrrrgh!" said Icky.

"EURRRRGH!" said Bryan.

"It looks like … brains!" gasped Icky.

"It *is* brains!" cried Bryan.

"Are you all right, Stinky?" asked Icky.

Stinky scratched his head, then looked down at his hands, much confused. "How can I be all right?" he replied. "I'm half left."

Icky breathed a sigh of relief. "Welcome back, Stinky," he said.

"I think," added Bryan, "it's time for a party."

The End Bit

Bryan, Icky and Stinky sat amongst the ruins of the wrapping-paper, tying up the loose ends.

"Wow," said Icky. "What a party."

"I'd like to describe it," said Stinky, "but it would be impossible to describe."

"You probably could describe it," said Icky, "if you still had your ten brains."

Stinky sighed. "I liked being clever," he said. "It was my deepest wish, and for a while it came true."

Icky became very serious. "You *can* be clever, Stinky," he said. "Like most people, you only use a tiny fraction of your brain. If you believe in yourself and work hard, you will be amazed at the results."

Note from Blue Soup:

Icky doesn't normally speak like this, as you know. However, they were being filmed for an educational TV special, and had been told to put little lessons into their stories.

"Sad to see Orfor go," said Stinky.

"He'll be fine," said Icky.

"I miss him," said Stinky.

"Yes," said Icky. "I'm glad we didn't eat him."

Stinky looked puzzled. "I thought we *did* eat him," he said.

"Nah," said Icky. "We ate the nut roast."

"We released Orfor back to his *natural habitat*," said Bryan.

"Oh good," said Stinky. "I think."

"Hey," said Icky. "Remember when we put the mirror down, and you did your bird-call, and we fooled him into thinking you were his mate!"

Everyone laughed.

"And remember when we had that Christmas pudding," said Bryan, "and all the insects came out of it!"

No one laughed.

"No, Bryan," said Icky. "That was your dream."

"Oh yes," said Bryan. He thought for a while, then his brow furrowed. "Hang on," he said. "How come you know what I dreamt?"

"Time for another game of Sardines!" said Icky. "I'll hide first!"

With that, Icky was gone, leaving Bryan hopelessly confused, but no more confused than usual in the ever-changing House of Fun.

Another title from Hodder Children's Books:

STINKY FINGER'S HOUSE OF FUN

Jon Blake

The Spoonheads have arrived in their space-hoovers and sucked up all the grown-ups! So Stinky Finger and Icky Bats will never have to change their underwear again.

In search of an Aim in Life, the two great mates head off to Uncle Nero's House of Fun. But soon they're being besieged by an army of pigs who want to make people pies!

They're going to need more than Icky's lucky feather and Stinky's smelly pants to save their crazy new home ...

Another title from Hodder Children's Books:

THE DEADLY SECRET OF DOROTHY W.

Jon Blake

When Jasmin wins a place at the Dorothy Wordsearch School for Gifted Young Writers, things look fishy. Who exactly is the mysterious Mr Collins?

How come Miss Birdshot, the wizened old housekeeper, is so incredibly strong?

And why do Jasmin's fellow pupils keep disappearing?

As Jasmin unravels Dorothy W.'s deadly secret, she finds herself literally writing for her life. Now, only the most brilliant story will help her survive!

'It's original and witty, full of amusing characterisation – a funny adventure story which credits its readers with intelligence.' Books for Keeps

Another title from Hodder Children's Books:

THE MAD MISSION OF JASMIN J.

Jon Blake

The last time Jasmin saw Dorothy Wordsearch, the awful author was being eaten by a monster.

So how come she's still writing stories?

It's time for Jasmin to investigate – helped, but mainly hindered, by her hyper sidekick Kevin Shilling.

And when Kevin is won over by a sinister new enemy, Jasmin will need all her wits to save him from a terrible fate …